THE FORCE AWAKENS

EGMONT
We bring stories to life

This edition first published in Great Britain 2017
by Egmont UK Limited, The Yellow Building,
1 Nicholas Road, London W11 4AN.

© & TM 2017 Lucasfilm Ltd.

ISBN 978 0 6035 7421 4
68485/1
Printed in Estonia

To find more great *Star Wars* books, visit www.egmont.co.uk/starwars

THE FORCE AWAKENS

Adapted by Christopher Nicholas
Illustrated by Caleb Meurer and Micky Rose

THIS BOOK BELONGS TO

A long time ago in a galaxy far, far away . . . .

Thirty years after the fall of the evil Empire, an army known as the First Order threatens to take over the galaxy. General Leia Organa, leader of the Resistance, needs help to restore peace. So Leia sends daring X-wing pilot Poe Dameron and his faithful droid BB-8 on a special mission to find a map that leads to her brother – Luke Skywalker, the last of the Jedi.

Poe and BB-8 travel to the planet Jakku, where they retrieve the map. Suddenly, the First Order attacks! Commander Kylo Ren and his stormtroopers capture Poe. Luckily, the pilot hid the map in BB-8.

BB-8 escapes into the desert. But the droid is soon trapped by an angry Teedo riding a luggabeast.

A young scavenger named Rey feels bad for the droid and rescues BB-8. Rey doesn't have a family, and BB-8 is clearly lost, so she agrees to let the droid stay with her.

Meanwhile, on board a First Order Star Destroyer, Kylo Ren uses the Force – a powerful energy field – to make Poe reveal that BB-8 has the map. The brave pilot is about to give up hope when he is rescued by a stormtrooper! FN-2187 doesn't want to fight for the First Order any more and offers to help Poe escape. They climb into a TIE fighter and blast off.

"I'm calling you Finn. That all right?" Poe says to FN-2187.

Just then, the Star Destroyer fires on the TIE, sending Poe and Finn crashing down to Jakku.

Finn can't find any sign of Poe among the TIE fighter wreckage. So he sets off and soon finds the pilot's droid and Rey at an outpost. Finn tells Rey about Poe and BB-8's special mission for the Resistance. Suddenly, stormtroopers appear and try to capture the trio!

Finn, Rey and BB-8 race aboard an old space freighter and blast off. First Order TIE fighters chase after them.

As Finn climbs into the gunner's seat, Rey pilots the freighter through an old Star Destroyer wreck. The heroes escape into space.

ZOOM!

Unfortunately, the freighter is damaged during the wild chase. Rey makes repairs while Finn asks BB-8 to reveal the location of the secret Resistance base. Suddenly, the freighter is caught in a tractor beam – and sucked into the cargo bay of a massive ship!

Rey, Finn and BB-8 hide under a grating.
But they are quickly discovered by a tall man and
a Wookiee. It is Han Solo and his co-pilot,
Chewbacca – heroes of the Rebel Alliance that
helped defeat the evil Empire
years ago!

"Chewie, we're home," Han
says to his furry friend. They
are thrilled to finally have their
stolen ship, the *Millennium
Falcon*, back again.

Rey and Finn are eager to deliver BB-8 and the map to the Resistance base. But first Han and Chewbacca have to deal with some uninvited guests – the Kanjiklub and the Guavian Death Gang!

Han owes both gangs money, and they are eager to collect.

Rey wants to help, so she tries to close the blast doors and trap the gangs. But instead she accidentally releases Han and Chewie's cargo – vicious creatures called rathtars! It is just the distraction Han and Chewbacca need to make their escape. Together with Rey, Finn and BB-8, they blast off in the *Falcon*.

Meanwhile, Kylo Ren returns to the stronghold of the First Order. Located on an ice planet, Starkiller Base is armed with a superweapon strong enough to destroy an entire solar system!

Kylo Ren reports to his master, Supreme Leader Snoke. "The droid we seek is aboard the *Millennium Falcon*, once again piloted by Han Solo," Snoke snarls.

Before flying to the Resistance
base, Han Solo lands on the planet
Takodana to get help from a friend. Maz is
a wise old alien who lives in a grand castle. Maz tries to give Rey
a special gift – Luke Skywalker's old lightsaber, a powerful laser
sword. But when she touches it, she has a vision of pain and suffering
and runs off. So Maz asks Finn to take the
lightsaber and keep it for Rey.

A spy in Maz's castle alerts Kylo Ren, and soon First Order stormtroopers attack!

The heroes put up a brave fight but Rey is captured by Kylo Ren and taken aboard his transport.

Suddenly, a squadron of Resistance
X-wing fighters – led by Poe Dameron –
zooms in and saves the day! Kylo Ren and his
troops retreat to Starkiller Base with Rey.

Back at the Resistance base, General Leia Organa and her team come up with a plan to destroy the Starkiller and rescue Rey. Han, Chewbacca and Finn fly the *Falcon* to the First Order base and sneak inside. The trio quickly disable the Starkiller's shields.

But as they try to find Rey's prison cell, they discover she has already escaped on her own. Reunited, the heroes begin placing explosive charges in the Starkiller's cooling system.

Suddenly, a dark figure appears! Kylo Ren removes his helmet – and reveals that he is really Han and Leia's son, Ben Solo! Han begs Ben to leave the First Order and come home with him. But Kylo Ren has been turned to evil by Supreme Leader Snoke. The villain ignites his red lightsaber and sends his father tumbling down into a deep pit!

Chewbacca fires his bowcaster, injuring Kylo Ren and giving the heroes a chance to escape.

As Rey and Finn race across the
frozen planet towards the *Falcon*, Kylo
Ren catches up with them! The villain
knocks Rey unconscious, but Finn
wields Luke Skywalker's lightsaber
to protect his friend.
Unfortunately, the former
stormtrooper is no match for Kylo
Ren and is quickly defeated.

But before Kylo Ren can deliver
the final blow, Rey awakens and
uses the Force to levitate the blue
lightsaber right into her hand!

With the Force as her ally, the young scavenger reveals herself to be a powerful warrior. The lightsaber battle comes to a sudden end when explosions create a deep crater between Rey and Kylo Ren.

Chewbacca flies in on the *Millennium Falcon* and helps Rey carry the injured Finn on board. The heroes blast off – just as Poe Dameron and his X-wing squadron fire their torpedoes at the Starkiller! The First Order's superweapon is destroyed!

KA-BOOM!

Back at the Resistance base, BB-8 projects the star map to Luke Skywalker's location. Unfortunately, a crucial part is missing. Luke Skywalker's old astromech droid, R2-D2, suddenly reactivates – and reveals the final piece of the map!

Rey and Chewbacca blast off in the *Millennium Falcon* and follow the map to a beautiful planet covered by blue water and green islands. They land on a mountain.

Rey climbs a stone staircase and meets a hooded figure. The figure lowers his hood, revealing the face of . . .

Luke Skywalker! Rey hands the Jedi Master his old lightsaber.

There has been an awakening in the Force – and young Rey knows that she has an exciting future ahead of her!

THE END